Cover Page

"For if you forgive men their trespasses, your heavenly Father will also forgive you. But if you do not forgive men their trespasses, neither will your Father forgive your trespasses." – Matthew 6:14, 15

Alicia

Chapter 1

"Hurry Santos, get in here the baby is coming!" Santos Rodriguez, a 20 year old very thin man with colorful tattoos running up both arms rushed into the delivery room in response to the urgent call of his young girlfriend's mother He came into the room just as the baby was crowning. He hurried to Renita Moore's side and squeezed her hand as the nurse screamed "puuuuuuuush!" for the last time. Renita shrieked triumphantly as the room filed with the cacophony of the baby's cries, well wishes from family members, and the hustled footsteps of nurses.

She was a 7lb 9 0z beautiful baby girl of 22 inches. Alicia Renee Moore. That was when things were good between her Mexican father and Black mother. Before Renita came up pregnant at 17, she and Santos were high school sweethearts who were ready to take on the world together. Santos blamed her and their new baby for taking him away from his dreams. He had always wanted to be a producer in the music industry and in his mind, having a slightly overweight girlfriend and a new baby girl to provide for was not going to get him recognized by the big wigs.

Santos began pulling further and further away from the family. He would tell Renita he was going to the studio every night but her womanly intuition told her he was cheating. Renita was never a woman to be walked all over so one lonely night she packed up her few belongings, grabbed the baby and left. She spent the night in the cheap motel that she and Santos used to sneak off to when they still lived with their parents back in high school. She kept hoping that he would show up to beg for her forgiveness. But he never did. He never even called to see where his family went.

After two days in the hotel she realized that she hadn't brought enough milk for Alicia. Renita took the baby with her and went back to the apartment to grab what they needed. She opened the door to a naked Santos. The furious scream she let out that day could be heard for miles. She gently placed little Alicia on the couch and immediately went to the bedroom where she discovered her best friend Amber lying on the bed. Feeling betrayed she seemingly gained extra human strength and flipped their mattress over to take all of the money that they had stuffed inside. It was just enough to get her a one way plane ticket to Harrisburg, Pennsylvania. Baby Alicia slept soundly all the way there.

Chapter 2

Alicia and her mom lived in government housing for a couple of years until Renita saved up enough money from her 3 minimum wage jobs to be able to afford a small house for rent on Pea street near downtown Harrisburg. The jobs still weren't enough so soon, Renita started selling herself sporadically any time she and her daughter needed extra money. Besides the occasional black eyes, bruised ribs, and lock jaw, tricking was profitable for a while until Renita came up pregnant again when Alicia was 12. She gave birth to a small baby boy whom she named Devin.

With Santos out of the picture many years before, neither Alicia nor Devin would ever get to know their dads very well. In fact Renita had only narrowed it down to 4 possibilities of who Devin's father actually was. Knowing that all this new baby boy had to depend on was his mother and sister, Renita slowed down with the prostitution to try to become the mother that her children would be proud of. She got herself a 9-5 secretarial job at a local law firm and worked weekends cleaning floors at the community college a couple blocks away from their house. Renita worked hard to make sure her children were fed and clothed and sent Devin to daycare while his sister started her last year of junior high.

Growing up Alicia had always been a quiet child, but Renita noticed that ever since Alicia entered junior high she was a bit more repressed than usual. Puberty was an extremely awkward time for Alicia because she was noticeably self-conscious about the fact that her chest wasn't growing as large as the other girls her age. None of the boy's wanted anything to do with her even though she would pine away for them. Renita suggested that Alicia should start straightening her hair and wearing makeup and fingernail polish so that she'd look more attractive to the boys she liked, but Alicia didn't want to hear that. She wanted her mom to tell her she was beautiful and perfect the way she was and that every boy should be begging to take her out on a date. Alicia resented her mother for the words she didn't say and she'd never fail to come home every day from school, say hello to her mother and brother, then lock herself in her bedroom until dinner time. Renita kept trying to get through to Alicia and finally one day she did. When Alicia told her mom that she wanted to go to her first school dance, the 8th grade spring spectacular, Renita leapt at the chance to make her little girl happy. She knew that Alicia was a good girl who stayed out of trouble and always kept her grades up, so the least she could do was buy her baby girl a new dress for her big night. But, after all the bills were paid and groceries were purchased there just wasn't enough ends to buy the new bright orange and white flowered Macy's dress that Alicia wanted. She didn't want to let her firstborn down, so Renita turned to a source of money she hadn't turned to in almost two years-prostitution.

"Mom, where are you going? It's almost 12 am and Devin is having nightmares again" said a sleepy Alicia stumbling from the small bedroom she shared with her little brother. "Go back to sleep, girl! I've got somewhere to go" Renita responded gently leading Alicia back to her room. As she walked, Renita's oversized jacket opened slightly and Alicia was able to see the short black skirt, blue crop top and fishnet stockings she was hiding underneath. Recognizing the choice of outfit on her 31 year old mother, Alicia rushed to the door, and blocked it with her slender body. "Mom I know what you are about to do, I thought you stopped doing that" she said with a look of hurt in her eyes. Renita looked down at her daughter, shamefaced. "Look Alicia, I need some extra money."

"No you don't Mom" Alicia pleaded, "we have enough food… and… and the lights are still on. Just stay home tonight. Please."

"Baby look I'll only be a couple of hours, I'm going to a safe part of the city… I - I've got a date" Renita stated as she pushed Alicia's small frame from in front of the doorway. "Imma get you that pretty dress you have been wanting for the dance. Don't you want to look nice baby?" she asked with a smile. With that Alicia fell silent as she dealt with the conflict of wanting to finally be noticed at school and wanting her mom to stay home. In her fourteen year old mind somehow she rationalized the act. 'Well she has a date, if the guy gives her some money what's wrong with that? I deserve to look good at the dance, I made the A honor roll three times in a row, Why can't I have fun?' With her mind partially at ease Alicia moved out of her mother's way completely and stammered a "be safe" before locking the door behind Renita. That was the last time she ever saw her mom.

Lady Lease

Chapter 3

A lot happened after Alicia's mom, Renita was strangled to death and left on the side of the road by the wealthy white man in the mysterious blue Cadillac. Eventually the cops found him and he plead not guilty by reason of insanity to a jury of his peers. Apparently nobody cared about the young woman he'd so viciously murdered or the two young children she'd left behind enough to fight for real justice. The man, her mom's murderer, now sat in a posh mental facility where he was allowed to make supervised trips to wherever he wanted to go essentially whenever he wanted to go. It is almost as if things were going better for him after he committed murder now that the taxpayers afforded a way for him to live rent free in his private room at the top floor of Ocean View Mental Institute. But, Alicia didn't have time to think about how comfortably her mom's murderer must be living- she had to figure out a way to keep her and her baby brother together.

She vividly remembered the day child protective services stormed into their little apartment on Pea Street talking about putting them up for adoption unless they could find a suitable guardian. She would have loved to stay with her grandmother Mary but she had died of cancer three years prior. Her biological dad was out- she didn't even remember meeting him. The only stories she heard about him were that he had nearly fainted in the delivery room the day she was born and that he once lost all their rent money on a bet on a basketball game. He and her mother broke up soon after her birth and he never became a music producer so he up and joined the Army. For all she knew he was probably married with children by now and that was fine with her. She wasn't going to beg a man to take her and her little brother in when he never wanted her to begin with. The coward could probably wield a gun in Afghanistan but was never interested in trying his hand at being a father to her.

Alicia racked her young brain and finally remembered Manny. Manny would surely take them in. He had moved to Brooklyn, New York, but when he lived in Pennsylvania he would come by the apartment every now and again to make sure the little family had enough food to eat. Manny was a drug dealer but at least he had a heart. She decided to call

Manny and see if he would take her and Devin into his home. Riiiiiiiiiiiiiiing Riiiiiiiiiiiiing Riiiiiiiiiiiiiinnnng Riiiiiiiiiiiiiinnnng…"Yo this is Manny you know what to do at the beep" blared the answering machine. "Hey Manny its Alicia, you know Renita's daughter? Well she died and now child protective serv-""Hey, hello? Alicia I'm here" Alicia relaxed as she heard Manny's baritone voice on the other end of the line. "Can you drive down here and tell these people you will take care of us? I can cook and clean for you and and and Dev he won't be any trouble at all, I'll watch him" Alicia stammered out over the phone. Apparently she and the promise of government cheese for supporting the kids was convincing enough for Manny because he was at their apartment door and signing the necessary paperwork before the night was over.

Manny was supposedly the man in New York so Alicia expected to pull up to a mansion in the city, but much to her dismay Manny's 2003 Honda civic slowed to a halt at a ratty old one story house in the middle of a narrow street. He must have spent all his money on the car. Alicia thought. "Alright yall welcome to my… ugh excuse me… welcome to our home sweet home" Manny announced proudly. "Ugh you might want to hurry up and get inside kids. I don't live in the best of neighborhoods" he chuckled. 'No you don't say thought Alicia sarcastically in her head.' With a shrug she scooped up little Devin and entered their new home. The fist night was the worst. First she discovered a dead baby cockroach intermingled in the noodles of her chicken spaghetti and then was forced to rock her little brother to sleep to the eerie lullaby of gunshots and helicopter blades.

Ever since her mom was murdered and she was ripped away from the pleasant life she'd known in Harrisburg, she found it hard to identify with kids her own age. She had a best friend in Pennsylvania but they hadn't really spoken since her mom's funeral. The conversations over the phone were always so strained and awkward now that they got fewer and farther in between. Now her best friend had become little Devin because, despite the large age gap, they had the sorrow of losing a mother in common and that was all the understanding that was needed.

Chapter 4

Going to school in Brooklyn was interesting to say the least. Alicia was shy and studious. All the people around her always seemed like they wanted to do things that she felt too mature for. Instead of participating in the rap battles in the hallways between classes or joining the onlookers of the occasional fights during lunch period she kept her nose in a good mystery book. Alicia was quite the loner. She never joined the crowd of gossiping girls or even the smoking group. But despite her lack of real friends, Alicia still got a lot of attention at school. In New York, It seemed like every other day a boy would ask for her phone number. Even though she would always decline their offers to hang out she could see the other girls seething with envy and could smell their jealousy like a shark smells blood. She knew that Brooklyn could be a dangerous city but she wasn't afraid.

The first and only time she got jumped was when she was walking home from school when she was near the end of her 9th grade when she had just turned 15. "Why come your hair look like that huh? You must think you better than us huh?" jeered Chantelle, the tallest 15 year old girl Alicia had ever seen. On account of her Mexican and black parentage, Alicia had luxurious long and curly locks that she would brush out every morning and let flow everyday at school. She thought it was her shining glory- her crown. Evidently the other girls felt the same way but instead of treating her like a princess they envied her. "O you deaf now? You aint gon answer me? I just wanna cut a piece of your pretty little hair" mocked Chantelle clutching a pair of scissors in her hand. Alicia didn't respond instead she turned around to walk the other way but was surprised to see two other angry looking girls hustling towards her. Never being one to back down, Alicia threw down her back pack and balled up her fists. "Hahaha oh that's cute! You really think you can take all of us?" Chantelle asked. After receiving no response all of the girls converged on the smaller girl at once but Alicia fought like a caged animal.

By the time she was finished all three girls were on the barren street bleeding. Alicia now held the scissors that Chantelle had been trying to cut her hair with and begin to walk towards the fallen girl. With the adrenaline still coursing through her tiny frame Alicia angrily raised her arms above her head ready to relieve all of her stresses on the body of her victimizer when someone forcefully grabbed her arm. " Yo ma I don't think you wanna do that" Alicia turned around to behold a handsome young lanky boy with caramel skin and almond shaped honey brown eyes that she would sometimes see around campus.

"I know you aint tryin to get arrested" he continued. Catching her breath, Alicia slowly lowered the weapon from above her head. "Thanks for stopping me, I probably woulda killed her" she admitted. "Well how bout we leave them stank girls here and ill walk you home Miss…" he paused "Alicia" she stated flatly finishing his sentence, "and you are?" "I'm Marcus he responded as he followed in the direction Alicia began walking. After walking together in silence for several minutes Marcus stopped and turned toward Alicia. "So you're the new girl and around here people gon hate on you." Alicia stared at him blankly as she waited for him to continue. "So basically what I'm trying to say is that you gon need protection, like you know, a family. We'll have your back and you'll have ours. I mean frankly I aint seen that kinda tenacity from a female in a long while lil mama" he said. Alicia had heard about gangs before but she had never thought about joining one, but now that Marcus had mentioned it, it would be nice for someone to have her back on these streets and it would be cool to hang out with people her own age since most of her free time was spent babysitting little Devin. "Yeah I see you and your clique hangin out on the corner. So what I gotta do to be down?" She asked. Marcus didn't answer right away. Instead he dug around in his backpack and pulled out a sheet of paper and an uncapped blue pen. On the paper he wrote down an address. "Come to this place if you want to… but let me warn you, this aint some little club, this is serious… this is a family." With that statement Marcus left Alicia standing in front of her doorstep wondering which direction she should go. "Hey Marcus wait up" she yelled and ran to catch up with him.

Chapter 5

The strong smell of weed mingled with the subtle smell of alcohol beginning to evaporate from skin greeted the two teenagers at the door of the trap house. "Sup Marcus" "Sup G" Marcus responded to the man as they dapped each other up. Big G was one of the most feared men on not just his block but the entire city. People said he got his nickname because he always knew what was going on in every corner of the city, almost like he was omnipresent. Or he could have gotten the name because of his 6 foot 5 inch 250 pound stature. "Yo Big G this is Alicia, she wants to be one of us." Marcus said. Big G looked Alicia up and down. "Alicia huh? Like Alicia Keys?" "Yeah" she answered quietly. "Well Alicia that's a sweet little name but how bout we call you Lady Lease, that cool with you?" "Yeah" Alicia answered again. "Well we gon take good care of you Lady Lease, and I promise after this you'll be our sister, but for now…" Big G stopped short looking around and licking his lips before continuing. "For now you just a fine lil female."

For the first time since entering the house Alicia looked around the smoky room and noticed five muscle- bound guys staring back at her. It was hard to tell their exact ages but she had seen two of them at the high school before and Big G looked like he was about 35. Looking uncomfortable, Marcus announced to the group that he had somewhere to go so he needed to leave. Before he left he asked if Alicia was sure she wanted to do this. After receiving her slight nod in the affirmative, Marcus exited the room and closed the door behind him. All of the guys converged on her petite but shapely figure at once. While it was happening she didn't scream nor did she cry. In her mind she made herself believe that this was a necessary step to getting to a better position in life. She wanted to believe that she was making a way for Devin. As much as she tried to not think, one thought did haunt her throughout the initiation. She couldn't help but wonder if her mom ever imagined that this would be the way her firstborn would lose her virginity. That was the only thing that bothered her. The pain of grown men taking turns inside of her body was minimal compared to the pain she had experienced when she lost her mother. If only she hadn't wanted that bright new dress to go to the 8th grade dance her mom would still be alive and she wouldn't have to be doing this to survive.

It was over quickly. When they were done the laughing and satisfied men left the room, one of them threw a roll of toilet tissue behind him so Alicia could clean herself up. After several minutes, Alicia emerged from the room with a slow unsteady gait. She was surprised to find that the guys who just moments earlier were behaving like ravenous beasts, were now calmly playing a game of NBA 2k2 live on the Xbox like nothing just happened. "Yo Lady Lease stay awhile, we got pizza in the fridge" said Big G rising to get her a slice. "Naw that's ok G I think I'll go home, I got school tomorrow" Alicia said stumbling out the door. "Hey you ok Lease?" Alicia turned toward the direction of the voice. "Yeah I'm straight" said a startled Alicia. "I thought you had left Marcus." "Naw girl I wasn't gonna leave you. If it woulda got too rough I woulda had your back." Alicia wondered how much rougher it had to get before he would have deemed it necessary to intervene. But, over the years Alicia saw that Marcus did, in fact, have her back. She couldn't count the number of times Marcus had gotten her out of trouble with the school principal with his smooth talking. "Look Ms. Brundage you know Alicia is a good girl. You don't have to suspend her again, listen I'll personally vouch for her that she won't sell anything else for the rest of the year. By the way Ms. Brundage, that's a nice dress." These meetings would always end the same. The 67 year old homely high school principal would get rosy cheeked and smile and say "ok, Marcus I trust you, I'll give your friend Alicia Moore one more chance… she is such a pretty girl…"

Chapter 6

Alicia had been down with the set for two years now. She had gotten tatted with their street number like all the other members a few months after she got in. She was naturally gifted in English and history so the brothers would always joke that if she was going to be their lawyer one day she couldn't have visible tattoos, so she decided to get hers in the middle of her back. Whenever any man took of her shirt they would know who she was affiliated with; not that she had been taking her shirt off for anybody. In fact she hadn't let a man touch her since being initiated. True to Big G's promise, the boys protected her like a sister. If any dude tried to holla he had to be approved by the crew first, and after that he would be monitored closely to make sure he was treating Alicia right. There were a lot more easy girls for 16 and 17 year old boys to penetrate so after awhile the boys just stopped talking to her altogether. It was too much work for them. The lack of distracting testosterone was good for Alicia though, so she didn't mind. By the time Alicia and Marcus were entering their senior year of high school, Alicia had a 3.9 GPA. Since she was so smart, especially in math, the gang had her handling all the finances. In exchange for her excellent services as accountant, her brothers made sure she had everything she wanted. And With Devin being five years old now he had a growing interest in sports and he wanted a lot. He loved watching basketball games on TV so he had to have the newest LeBron's and he was playing in a local t-ball league so he had to have the freshest cleats, all sponsored by her family. It was good for her and Devin that she had them because Manny hadn't really been able to find legitimate work since he was busted for carrying an un- licensed gun and went to jail for a year when she was 16. During that year seemingly everybody she knew would let her and Devin crash for a few nights, but she spent most of her time with Marcus and his family. Marcus had two overweight little brothers who were only 5 and 3, but ate like boys going through puberty. There was never much food available in the single parent home but there was enough love to make up for it. Alicia respected the way Marcus's mom, Angie still instilled the values of discipline and responsibility in her boys even though there wasn't a man around to help her do that. Marcus's dad and her husband was killed by a stray bullet as he was coming home from his post office job just a couple months after their youngest son was born. Marcus and Alicia had a profound connection because they both understood the pain, anger, and guilt that came from losing a parent so soon. Alicia knew that like her, the loss of one of his parents drew him to seek the male leadership that a child so desperately needs in other places. That father for him was Big G. Marcus would cross the Sahara desert in an astronaut suit if G wanted him to. That type of loyalty was infectious and Alicia found herself becoming more and more loyal to Marcus.

One time whenever they were 17, Marcus asked her to deliver some drugs for him on the west side of the city. "I can't go over there Lease", he said. "You know that's where the enemy stay."

"Yeah I do so what makes you think they won't try to shoot me too?" Alicia asked.

"Cuz you too sexy girl" Marcus laughed as a Alicia rolled her eyes at him. "Plus me and Rondo just jumped one of they homeboys for coming to our block so I know if they see me it's gonna be on sight."

"What so you scared now?" Alicia asked playfully. "Naw I just don't wanna swell my hands up again" he laughed.

"Fine whatever give me the work" Alicia said after sucking her teeth at him.

Because of all the runs she had been doing for Marcus for years, by the time her senior year rolled around she had become proficient in being discreet with the drugs she was selling. After her couple slip ups her sophomore year with Principal Brundage, she never once got caught. She mostly sold weed, but occasionally she'd graduate to cocaine. School was busy for her since she was on the block on the weekends and taking advanced placement classes during the weekdays, so she was ready just to have some fun and enjoy the senior prom. Alicia avoided going to the prom her junior year because she felt like going to a school dance was too reminiscent of the night her mother was killed. It was actually Marcus who talked her into going to the senior prom.

"Yo you know it's not your fault right? What happened to your moms." Marcus said after she expressed her plan to miss the prom just as she did the year earlier. "Plus imma be there so you know it's gonna be a good time" Marcus continued.

"What makes you think I wanna hang out with you?" Alicia asked smiling.

"Well number one my dashing good looks and number

two you know every dude in that school is too scared to talk to you so it looks like I'm your only hope" "Can't argue with you there… except with the first statement" she said. It didn't take much convincing for her to go to the prom. It seemed like when it came to Marcus he could convince her to do anything. They went shopping for a prom dress that night before the mall closed.

Alicia found Marcus attractive but she never wanted to cross the line with him since they had such a close friendship but she did have her eye on another guy. His name was Victor and he was the newest member of los víboras. Unfortunately they were her sets main rival, but she couldn't deny Victor's striking good looks. He was Puerto Rican and he had a sexy accent. His dark brown skin contrasted perfectly with his hazel eyes and perfectly straight white teeth. To complement his easy smile he had a chiseled body that he managed to show off as often as possible by wearing sleeveless shirts. He was hot, no doubt about it but he was off limits, he was the enemy. After confiding in Marcus about maybe starting a Romeo and Juliet type romance with Victor and receiving a speech on loyalty in return, Alicia resigned to the fact that Victor would just remain eye candy.

The evening of the prom came and Alicia was picked up by Marcus in his freshly washed vanilla 98 Cadillac at 6pm sharp. The pair looked stunning. She in a strapless mandarin orange gown, and he in a white tuxedo with an orange vest, and some orange alligator shoes. Fresh. At first the pair only danced to fast songs together but finally getting bold Marcus asked Alicia to dance to a slow song, a favorite of hers, Adorn by Miguel. As the R&B crooner poured his heart out over the record Alicia and Marcus found themselves being drawn closer and closer to one another. Alicia rested her head lightly upon his shoulder. "Whoa what's that?" exclaimed Alicia as she felt a solid bulge pressing against her groin area. Marcus jumped back with an embarrassed look on his face. "Ugh I'm sorry Lease" Marcus said uncomfortably. "It's no big deal" Alicia assured him as she choked back her laughter. "I just think I'm just gonna go outside to get some air."

Alicia stepped outside feeling a little weird. She didn't think her and Marcus were anything but friends. Sure he was attractive, but just like Victor there were some lines you just shouldn't cross. A few moments after Alicia went outside, Victor joined her. "What's up mamacita? You look real good tonight mami" Alicia was flattered because Victor could get any girl at school but here he was complimenting her. "Thanks" she responded, "but you know you and I can't do anything you know who I roll with she said turning slightly so he could see the top part of her back tattoo. "Oh I know "laughed Victor, "but I seen the way you been checkin me out. But I aint tryin to start no war" said Victor staring out at the street. "Hey how bout we just go for a stroll" he suggested after a few moments.

He made her comfortable by keeping his distance and keeping the conversation light. "So I was thinkin, maybe we could catch a movie or somethin on the upper eastside. You know mami outside of both our territories" Victor said coyly. "Well let me think about it, but let's just walk for now" Alicia said smiling. She let her guard down and forgot her training. She allowed Victor to walk her around a corner to the side of the school where the outdoor bathrooms were. 'If he gets too frisky, I'll just hit him with a two piece and run' Alicia thought. She wasn't gonna give it up to him but she didn't mind if they kissed a little bit. "Come on in here Alicia" Victor beckoned gently as he stepped into the vacant men's bathroom. Those beautiful hazel eyes drew her in. Their lips met as Victor ca-ressed her back in his strong hands.

About a minute into the pleasant make out session, Victor grabbed her butt and began to zip down her strapless dress. Alicia pulled away quickly and told Victor to stop. When he didn't she reared back and hit Victor with a right cross. But even though she could fight, Alicia underestimated Victor's strength. He grabbed her by the waist turned her around roughly and slammed her to the cold floor of the empty restroom. 'Please someone come in!' Alicia pleaded in her head. She began screaming as loudly as she could but that just made Victor press her face into the filthy blue tile even harder. She soon ran out of the strength to fight him. With leopard like speed he had hiked up the skirt of her dress, pushed aside her panties and inserted himself. It seemed like it lasted for hours. He just kept panting and moaning, moaning and panting.

When he finally got off of her, he yelled "I was never feelin
you mami. It was a dare that I couldn't smash. Hahahahaha
7th in the class hah! I guess you're not that smart after all."
And with that Victor pissed on her back covering her tattoo
completely with his smelly urine and left the restroom laughing. Alicia got up off the floor, wiped herself off and stumbled
out of the restroom crying hysterically. She heard Marcus
yelling her name. "I'm over here Marcus "Alicia yelled back
through her sobs. Marcus ran over to where she stood and
immediately gasped when he saw her appearance. Already as-
suming the worst Marcus's eyes turned to ice as he asked what
happened to her. "Vic… Vic" Alicia began. That was
enough for Marcus. He ran to his car and started the engine
while he fumbled with the glove box key in order to get his
glock. The sound of tires screeching was deafening as Alicia
watched him speed off into the night.

Chapter 7

Marcus rolled up to Victor's house as quietly as he could,
with the headlights off, engine softly purring. Marcus was in
enemy territory off of 15th street, part of the 5 block radius of
los víboras. Marcus sat in the car squinting his eyes to see if
anybody was milling around in the darkness outside of Victor's
house. He saw no one. "Where is that son of a …" Marcus
stopped midsentence as he reacted to a noise outside. As he
searched for the sound he realized that he was staring down
the barrel of Victor's 22 just outside of his passenger window.
Without hesitation Victor angled the pistol down and fired two
rounds through the glass. The bullets ripped through Marcus's
flesh. With a yelp Marcus stepped on the gas pedal. 'Just get
home, just get home,' he thought. Marcus fumbled with his
cell phone as he drove. A torrent of blood saturated his white
tuxedo shirt and his eyes begun to flutter as he neared his
house.
　　"Marcus! Marcus!" Alicia's sweet voice snapped his eyes
back open. Alicia ran to the car, opened up the door and slid
in the passenger seat allowing Marcus to rest his head on
her lap. "When you didn't answer your phone I went to your
house and called 911. They're on their way… Stay with me."

Alicia pleaded as her eyes filled with tears. "Alicia you gotta tell me something." Marcus paused. "Did you ever think of me as more than a friend?" He asked. "Yes" Alicia sniffed trying to keep her emotions in check. "I...I love you Marcus" she said looking him full in the face. Marcus smiled and opened his mouth to respond. But where sweet words of affirmation were supposed to proceed, dark red blood gurgled out. Marcus panicked clawing wildly as death began to overtake him. He took his last breath just as the paramedics arrived. Not seeing the point of controlling her emotions any longer, Alicia let her tears rain down.

The whole city was in turmoil after Marcus's murder. Big G vowed to not only kill Victor but anyone who loved Victor. But Victor was long gone. He must have taken off soon after firing those two fatal shots. The coward didn't even bother to take his ailing grandmother and little sister with him. For his inconsiderate mistake they were now resting in peace 6ft under thanks to Big G. In war there were no rules. The sirens of ambulances and the sounds of lazy witness interviews by uninterested policeman were a perpetual nightmare. With one week left of high school and two days after Marcus's murder, she went to the Ms. Brundage's office and informed her that she would be absent for the rest of the week and that she would need her diploma mailed to her as she would not be attending graduation. Knowing how close Alicia and Marcus were, Ms. Brundage completely understood. "Where will you go?" Ms. Brundage asked with a concerned look on her face. "Far away from here." Alicia responded and quickly left the office. She wasn't in the mood for a counseling session. She didn't want the awkward stares and questions from staff and nosy students. She wanted to forget the whole situation. She wanted to forget that she had truly loved someone and waited to tell him just before he was ripped away from her forever. She wanted to forget that Marcus Thompson had ever existed. It was time for a new start. That meant breaking all ties with the gang. She understood that unlike other gangs whose policy was death is the only way out, her family allowed for one to be uninitiated in the same manner they were initiated. The only problem was she was a woman and she hadn't been jumped in. She shuddered at the thought of being uninitiated.

Big G understood. While he wouldn't let her officially leave the gang without being uninitiated, he and the rest of the brothers agreed to let her take a break for as long as she needed. They would always be her family but just as the mama bird has to let her chick leave the nest, it was now time to let their little sister go out and find her wings.

Alicia didn't feel like being around anymore killing, or gunfire, or fighting and a large piece of her heart died along with Marcus that dread filled night a week ago. She needed to go somewhere unfamiliar to start anew. Just her and little Devin. Manny was too old to make a drastic change in his life because he was still a prisoner of the old mentality. But Devin, Devin was just a child; A clean slate, still innocent. This wicked environment hadn't corrupted his pure mind yet. Alicia understood why she always heard that Jesus loves the little children. And from that day forward she vowed to keep her brother pure and innocent. She vowed to never trust another man. She vowed to never fall in love again.

Texas. Austin, Texas. The city of music, and the state where everything is bigger. 'Austin, TX, will be our new home,' Alicia thought as she gazed at the map of America in the 11th grade U.S history book she had kept. She and Devin packed a few bags, said goodbye and thank you to Manny and hopped on a plane that same day. Due to her previous employment as a lucrative drug supplier, and with a couple grand in parting gifts from Big G she had enough cash to keep her and Devin afloat for a few months. She rented a small apartment near Huston Tillotson College. She could have afforded a place in a nicer area but she had to be smart with her cash since she hadn't procured a job just yet. After about a solid month on the job hunt Alicia still hadn't found anything that interested her, so fast food it was.

She worked the day shift at Wendy's while Devin went to his new elementary school. Alicia had never had a legal job before so working at Wendy's was interesting to say the least. Dealing with a fat guy in a red shirt always telling her to mop the greasy floor, take out the smelly garbage, and to smile a little bit wider at the customers was quite foreign to her. She enjoyed getting away from the normalcy of the street life but if one more impatient customer asked her "uh is my food done yet?!" she was gonna spazz out! But, One day during the short bus ride home from work she felt a ray of hope that maybe she and Devin would make it. That sunlight came in the form of a billboard advertising the police academy. 'Don't police officer's get to fight, shoot guns, and intimidate people?' Alicia thought. 'Well sounds like a job for me' she wordlessly continued. She stepped into her and Devin's little apartment with a new lease on life. She knew being a cop was frowned upon in the hood but she couldn't deal with the fast food minimum wage grind, and she didn't feel like college was the right place for her either. Never one to let things lull, she applied to the police academy that same week.

Officer Moore

Chapter 8

"Hey my names Brian" said an unfamiliar face taking a seat next to Alicia. "Hey" Alicia responded nonchalantly. "Well are you going to tell me your name or do I have to look at your paper to find it out" the man continued. Rolling her eyes Alicia properly introduced herself to him. Brian made small talk with her until the instructor came in and began class. For some reason Alicia couldn't focus on the lecture though it was an interesting topic. Maybe her lack of focus stemmed from the delicious thought of Brian's soft wide set lips, chocolate skin, and deep brown eyes. The way his arm muscles threatened to bulge out of his long sleave shirt didn't hurt either. "Snap out of it Lease!" Alicia shouted mistakenly out loud. "What was that Alicia?" the instructor asked. "Nothing" an embarrassed Alicia muttered. She shyly glanced over at Brian to see his reaction and was dazzled by one of the best smiles she'd ever seen. 'Boy this is gonna be a long 6 months' Alicia thought, then quickly looked around to make sure she didn't accidently say it aloud.

Getting through class was rough seeing as how she didn't want to be involved with a man again but just happened to be sitting next to the best looking guy she had seen in a while. She did however manage to pick up on some suggestions given in class for how to properly handle traumatic experiences. One of the simplest suggestions that she wanted to try was journaling. The instructor had encouraged the class to go buy a special notebook of some sort and write down all major experiences they have had in their life whether good or bad. That sounded like a good idea to Alicia since she had never divulged many of her internal struggles to anybody. The only one she had ever told about her feeling responsible for the death of her mother was Marcus and now he to, was gone. In fact she hadn't even filed a police report against Victor for raping her. She had assumed it would be handled on the street. Victor though had seemingly vanished, but maybe one day she would get the chance to exact the revenge that she desperately needed. But for now she would have to find her solace in a journal. She decided on a red leather bound journal with gold rimmed russet pages. These pages would

be her closest confidant until the hole in her heart finally
healed. She wrote religiously in her journal everyday for the
5 remaining months in the academy. Though Devin was still
too young to understand much of what she had written, she
didn't want him to stumble upon the journal. She didn't take
any chances so she locked it up in her strong box next to her
academy issued 22.

Ten Years Later

Chapter 9

Alicia had blossomed into a beautiful woman. She had
the slender figure of her youth but now stood at 5 foot 5 with
a tiny waist, medium sized hips and size C cups that's seemed
to spring up overnight. She still wore her hair curly, but since
it had grown more than six inches since she was young she
wore her hair up in a tight bun most of the time. Although she
still didn't consider herself a girly girl she enjoyed experiment-
ing with different eye shadows and lip liners on weekends she
was off of work. She still had a firm policy against wearing
nail polish, however.

By now Alicia was established in her career as Officer
Moore. She had been working her beat at the University of
Texas at Austin for 8 years now. She loved everything about
the youthful environment, everything except for the occasional freshman knuckleheads that would call her Mrs. Officer
and beg her to arrest them. "See the damage that lil Wayne
has done?" she would always respond with a chuckle. Truth
be told they were a great source of entertainment for her and
her veteran partner William Hill. William was a sweet man,
dedicated to the force, and an all around stand up guy. He
only had one major flaw- he was terribly boring. How many
stories about his year old granddaughter could he tell? The
little girl couldn't even put together full sentences yet. This
was Alicia's perpetual thought as she could always count on
a story or two about "wittle Gracie" every time they came
together for an eight hour shift.

Though she got along well with William she was excited
when he announced his retirement in their weekly unit meeting. "Well I guess that means we gotta find you a better part-

ner Alicia" the captain joked. Alicia smiled along with the rest of the room as kind stories were shared about William and the 35 years he had spent in service. She hoped whoever replaced William was just as respectful and dedicated as he had been. A rap on the door awoke everyone out of their nostalgia as the eyes in the room shifted to the half opened door. "Sorry sir for interrupting your meeting, but I was just transferred to this unit and told that I should come here to meet my new partner" an unmistakably deep sexy voice said. "Well Officer Brian Simms welcome aboard!" The Captain heartily greeted Brian while shaking his hand and clapping him on the back. "You'll find your partner right there, "he said pointing to the middle of the room "name's Alicia Moore."

Alicia was now 27 and Devin was 15. He was growing up to be a handsome young man and unfortunately he knew it. He was just as athletic as he was when he was younger, but now he was lifting weights pretty often. Sometimes after school he'd come home and tell Alicia that all the girls said that he looked like a young Trey Songz. In addition to his inflated ego, Devin was getting a little tougher to handle than he used to be. Devin used to do anything Alicia asked of him and he was always very respectful but as of late he wasn't listening to her. Alicia expected it was because he had gotten himself some skirts. It was as if he thought that penetrating some hormone raged teenage girl made him a man. Well at least Alicia didn't have to worry about Devin not liking any of her boyfriends, because she hadn't had a boyfriend since moving to Austin. Sure she would catch a movie or a meal with the opposite sex every now and then but she would never bring them home. Whenever it seemed like a man was getting to close to her body or her heart was getting to close to him she'd simply stop going out with the gentleman. The excuse that she had to work double shifts all week usually got her point across to her courters. But her new partner and secret academy crush Brian was a different story. He was always professional when they were on their shift together but after they both clocked out he never failed to casually invite her out to watch the game or to get a smoothie, or go for a walk. And she never failed to tell him no. She just couldn't take the chance of falling for this guy. She never confessed

this to anyone except her journal but she had fantasies about
the man at night. Too often she woke herself up from moaning
in her sleep. She didn't worry about Devin hearing her
because they both slept with their room doors closed and
Devin would crank up his Tupac music every night when
he slept. Though her little brother couldn't hear her she was
nonetheless frustrated that a man had consumed her dreams.
The last guy she had lusted for had raped her due to her na-
ivety. She needed to stay stoic in Brian's presence. She didn't
want him to think that he had a chance with her, and she
certainly didn't want to show any weakness. From past experience opening her heart to someone was just that- weakness.

Chapter 10

During an uneventful day at the campus Alicia found
herself conversing easily with Brian. This was odd because
usually there was so much sexual tension from her that their
conversations were often brief and superficial. For Alicia it
was always so weird looking Brian full in the face knowing
that the night before she was imagining him pleasuring her
until the wee hours of the morning. But something was different about today. Maybe it was the beautiful spring day or the
playful attitudes of the little squirrels that were playing hide
and go seek around a tree near their car. Or maybe it was just
time.

"So Brian, tell me about your childhood" Alicia started.
Pleased that they were having a deeper conversation than
they usually had, Brian smiled as he explained that he was
an Army Brat and he had lived in 5 different states but called
Austin home since he graduated from high school in Texas.
Alicia thoroughly enjoyed being regaled by stories of his
high school football career and his embarrassing attempts at
singing in junior high. The stories eventually came to an end
and it was her turn to share. Alicia considered starting from
the night her mother was murdered, but decided against it as
she didn't want to be pitied. Instead she told Brian about the
few comical stories she remembered from elementary school.

Alicia assumed that Brian would try to prod her for more information about her life but much to her chagrin he didn't dig deeper. He seemed to be enjoying himself equally as much as she was. She didn't remember a man other than Marcus or her former partner who never asked her to do anything more than what she wanted to do. That made her comfortable. Before the end of the shift she opened up a little bit about the struggles she had been having with Devin. "Devin… is that your boyfriend?" Brian asked confused. "Ha ha ha no no that's my little brother remember? That's why I lived separately at the academy" Alicia assured him. "He is 15 now and he's starting to think he's grown." "Oh yeah I remember that you lived separately, but I thought that was your son" Brian said. "Until just now you thought I had a teenaged son and you were still checkin for me?" Alicia asked with amazement. "Well I believe in not holding someone's past against them" Brian answered tenderly looking Alicia deep in her eyes. Sensing her growing uncomfortableness, Brian quickly changed the subject back to Devin. "So you say Devin's been thinkin hes grown huh? Probably caught Adam's syndrome." "Adam's syndrome? Whats that?" Alicia questioned. Laughing Brian said "Well it's when a boy gets his first taste of the nectar. Once he's tasted it he is willing to disobey all authority even God Himself, so don't take it personally. He's just a little whipped right now" Brian laughed.

After the shift Alicia walked in the apartment noticeably bubblier than usual. "What's up with you sis?" Devin asked. "Nothing" Alicia responded. "I just had a pretty good day at work." "Well whatever as long as it don't got nothing to do with a man I'm straight" Devin said jokingly but he was probably serious. "So I see you got your bags packed Dev… where do you think you're going?"

Alicia asked folding her arms across her chest. "Oh I'm gonna spend the weekend with my girl Rhonda. Her parents are going to South Padre Island this weekend so she's gonna be all al… er well she wanted somebody there to look out for her ya know?" Devin stammered.

Alicia put her hands on her hips and prepared for battle. "Boy do you think I'm stupid, that's a booty call if I aint never seen one!" Alicia replied. "Oh yeah you would know aaaaaaallllllllllllllllll about that Alicia" Devin said under his breath. "What did you say?!" Alicia inquired loudly. Devin repeated what he said this time more brazenly. "Oh don't try to talk about things you know nothing about little boy! I know what is best for you and screwing that little girl all weekend is not it!" Alicia yelled with finality. She turned to walk away as Devin responded. "You have some nerve trying to preach to somebody about not screwing LADY LEASE! O yeah I read in your little journal about how you let 6 guys do you at once" Alicia gasped. "You know until I stumbled upon your journal when I was trying to find my sock in the laundry basket in your room, I thought you was a virgin?!" But you just tryin to slow ME down now. You already did your dirt, sold your drugs, and let everyone hit that wanted to… at least Rhonda's my girlfriend." Devin spat. "Shut up Devin … you have no idea what you are talking about. How much of that did you read?" Alicia asked slowly trying to decrease her heart rate and calm down. "O I read enough" Devin answered. "Here you are trying to call the shots, but you aint my momma. And you should feel guilty for her death. If it wasn't for you momma would still be here and maybe she could tell me to stay home this weekend!"

With that last tirade Devin turned from his sister to get some granola bars from the pantry. After a few moments Alicia broke the tense silence that filled the small kitchen. "Take your crap and get out of my house" Alicia stated flatly. With that she walked to her bedroom and shut the door. Alicia had become a master at hiding her feelings. She would wait until the front door slammed signaling Devin's departure before she let the flood gates open and the screams of anguish loose that were sure to follow.

It seemed like it took hours for Alicia's tear ducts to stop leaking. She needed to talk to someone, but she felt like she had no one. Marcus was dead, Manny was now an addict, and since the last time she talked to them over ten years ago, she didn't associate with Big G or the brothers anymore. She found her fingers absent mindedly flipping the pages of the local phone book. Her active fingers stopped turning pages when she reached the "s" section. She skimmed the section for Simms. Brian Simms. Before she could talk herself out of it she found her fingers dialing his home number. He answered

on the second ring. "Hello…. hello….hello anybody there?"
Brian asked in his patient velvety smooth voice. "It's me."
Alicia answered her voice and body weary. "Where are you?"
Brian asked. "At my apartment, Ballpark on Riverside Drive,
Apartment 223." "I'll be right over" Brian responded. "Ok…
but no funny business remember I gotta gun" Alicia said not
fully wanting to let her guard down. "So do I" Brian laughed
before hanging up the phone.

It only took Brian about 10 minutes to get to her apartment. It was impressive seeing as though the phone book
listed him as living north of the University which was about
20 minutes from Riverside. 'He must have turned on the si-
ren'. Alicia thought rising in response to the knock at the door.
"Come on in" Alicia said with uncertainty as she opened the
door and stepped aside for Brian's 6 foot 3 frame to enter.
After a few moments of awkward silence, Alicia opened her
mouth to speak, but no words came out. She felt silly for in-
viting this man over. Why did she even invite him over in the
first place? It wasn't like they had been close in the academy
but their talk earlier made her a lot more comfortable.

Brian slowly walked over to Alicia, assuring her that no
words needed to be spoken. Like a father and a lover at the
same time Brian wrapped his strong arms around her and
Alicia buried her head into his chest. Seemingly thousands
of thoughts raced through her mind at once. It was all quite
overwhelming for her. She really just wanted to scream but
was too afraid of fully opening herself up to him. The only
other man she had cried in front of was Marcus as he was
dying.

She had years and years of pressure in the form of
despair held in her hardened heart. Maybe her heart wasn't
as calloused as she thought because now in this moment she
felt more human than ever and in this man's arm she felt more
loved than ever. All at once she let herself go. She began to
shake, scream, and cry like she had never done before. Brian
stood steady allowing Alicia to beat his chest with her balled
up fist as she screamed and clutched his back with her other
hand. All her guilt, shame and fear boiled up to the forefront
of her brain. Every single gunshot she grew up with, her mother's death, and Devin's betrayal replayed in her mind. Her

controlled tantrum went on for five minutes. She was exhaust-
ed. With Alicia still sniffling lightly Brian gently stroked her
untied curly hair picked her up in his warm embrace and laid
her on the couch in the front room and lay down beside her.

Alicia awoke several hours later to dried snot under her
nose and Brian's arm around her waist. She leapt up quickly
waking Brian up. "Look Brian um I think you need to leave"
she said wiping her nose with a Kleenex from the box on the
ottoman. Brian looked confused. "Get up now!" Alicia continued with venom in her voice. Wordlessly Brian put back
on the light brown timberland boots he had taken off before
laying next to Alicia on the couch. Brian made his way to the
door without a sound. As he neared the door, Alicia began to
cry. She was frustrated at how she was behaving. One minute
she was angry and independent, the next she was sad and
lonely. Brian turned away from the door and cradled Alicia's
face in his hands. "Alicia I'm not going anywhere. I really
consider you a friend and you need my help. You can yell
at me all you want but I'm not leaving you." With that Brian
walked back to the couch and sat down firmly planting his
feet on the floor with a patient look on his face. After a couple
more of her "leave right now" commands were ignored by
Brian, Alicia finally moved away from the door and joined
Brian on the couch. They sat in silence. "Ok so I'm ready to
talk now" Alicia blurted out unable to stand the silence any
longer. "I'm all ears" Brian responded. "Well it all started
when I was fourteen…when I lost my mom…" Alicia began.
She and Brian talked for hours, with Alicia doing most of the
talking. For the first time in a long time Alicia felt safe sharing
her inner thoughts with someone. With everything now out
in the open she began to get aroused. As Brian talked about
how he knew everything would turn out alright for her, Alicia
rubbed her hands gently down Brian's torso, allowing a hand
to linger around his groin area. Brian stopped midsentence
visibly taken aback. Alicia took his sudden silence as a con-
firmation that he was feeling the same thing she was and she
leaned in to kiss him. Brian backed away to avoid the kiss and
removed her hands from his body. "Uh I gotta go Alicia. Take
care" Brian said abruptly rushing out the door. Alicia locked
the door back very confused as to what just happened.

Chapter 11

It was Monday now and Brian and Alicia were together again at their post on speedway at the University of Texas campus. Conversation was a bit strained despite the sob session they had shared on the previous weekend. Alicia was embarrassed at the diarrhea of the mouth that caused her to spill all the secrets that she had told no one except for her red leather journal. She just felt so comfortable in that moment on the couch with Brian. He was such a great listener. He didn't interrupt her and try to fix all her problems like most men tend to do. He was merely being a friend. She was also pleasantly surprised that he didn't take advantage of her weakened state and try to sleep with her. Of course, that only made Alicia burn more for him sexually. Truth be told she would have let him if he had asked. Brian not accepting her advances not only made her more attracted to him, but also it made her suspicious. This incredibly attractive man had a golden opportunity to get some booty and he hadn't taken it. Either she had lost a step or he was a flaming homosexual. There was no other explanation.

Against all standards of political correctness Alicia asked Brian what had been on her mind since that Saturday evening. "Brian are you gay?" Alicia asked. Much to Alicia's surprise, Brian busted out in raucous laughter. "No Alicia I'm not gay" Brian answered her once his uncomfortable laughter died down. "Alicia especially after everything you had just told me I definitely didn't want to take advantage of you like those other guys did. Besides I'm saving myself for the woman I will marry." "Pardon me but what are you saying?" Alicia asked with a quizzical look on her face. "Well if I must spell it out in plain English to you, I am a virgin and I will remain a virgin until I get married" Brian answered. "Hahahahaha whatever boy! We both know you and your fine self is not no virgin!" Alicia said. "Oh so you think I'm fine huh?" asked Brian with a lopsided grin. "Well let's not change the subject we are talking about you not me mister" Alicia stated. "Ok fair enough Alicia I'll keep this about me. Yes I've never had sex before with anyone because I take the Bible at face value and I believe that because I have a relationship with Jesus Christ I should keep it in my pants until I get married like the Bible commands me to. Yes it has been very hard for me to stay that way for 28 years. I've had my close calls...."Brian stopped "I'm listening" Alicia encouraged him to keep going. "Well truth is I've had my close calls in the past... so close that the condom was already on." Brian laughed. "What I'm trying to say is if I started with you I probably wouldn't be able to stop. I find you incredibly beautiful and alluring. I mean you're intelligent, charismatic and funny. To be honest with you, you are the last one on my mind at night and I have to fight off thoughts of us making love over and over again in my dreams all the time" Brian finished staring Alicia deep in her eyes. That confession caught Alicia totally off guard. Yet again she was speechless in his presence. "Say something Alicia" Brian urged. Alicia began to squeak out a response just as the radio screeched on.

"Possible fire by the tower all available units in the area please respond." Alicia drove around to Campus Circle behind the tower relieved for the work related change of subject. Both officers stepped out of the car to check the area and find the problem. Fortunately there was no serious issue. It was just a bored student pulling the fire alarm for kicks. Alicia shuddered at the thought of the sizable fine the student would be forced to pay for the expense of the first respond-ers responding to the false alarm. After the firefighters and paramedics cleared the scene it was time for Brian and Alicia to head back to their post. Alicia would finally have to share her feelings for Brian as well. 'Please have another call please have another call' Alicia repeatedly plead in her mind looking at the radio in the car. There was no other call on the radio. Seeing that she would receive no interruption from work, Alicia decided it would be best to get this possible awkward moment out of the way.

"I promised myself I would never again feel this way about another man but holding my feelings back backfired on me once before so I figured I should just be all the way honest with myself and you." Alicia said staring out the window. "Hey Mrs. Officer would you please arrest me?" pleaded a short boy through the half opened window interrupting the moment. By the time she opened the door to respond he had taken off around the corner leaving behind him a scattered group of giggling passerby. "Kid's these days..." Alicia said shaking her head and closing the car door.

Alicia drove back to the station at the end of the shift. After the interruption by the hormonal teenager the conversation stayed superficial for the remaining two hours left on the clock. "See ya tomorrow" Alicia said to Brian hanging back in the station trying to avoid walking outside to their cars together. "Peace" answered Brian quickly exiting the building seemingly trying to avoid the same thing.

Alicia wandered back to the Captain's office and allowed herself to linger in the shadows. "So Cap we got to get the dudes" "Well the only way to bust them is to get a mole in there" Alicia overheard the Captain and His second in command talking. Deciding not to eavesdrop any longer, Alicia began to walk away until one name made her ears perk up- los víboras. "Um I'm sorry to interrupt Captain but I couldn't help but overhear what yall were talking about" go on the captain responded "Well" Alicia continued, "I could be your mole. I have er... well let's just say I have considerable experience in that area" Alicia finished. "What type of experience?" the captain inquired. "I don't remember reading that you had done any undercover work in your file Alicia." "Well sir, it's not in my file but I guarantee you that I have firsthand experience with that gang" Alicia assured the captain. "As you know, I grew up in Brooklyn New, York"

She explained that she had attended high school with some of the members of los víboras but she didn't tell him everything. She didn't want to tell the captain that she was a sworn enemy of the gang, because she knew that not only would the captain deem it a conflict of interest for her to be involved in the case but he would probably get her kicked out of the force altogether. "Well Alicia you're a good cop, dedicated, responsible and intelligent. We will have to review your file and we will get back to you within the week" the captain said. "Yes sir, I look forward to the call" Alicia assured them leaving the office. Alicia had never really prayed before but she prayed now. "Please God let me get this job" she said looking up at the ceiling. She was fueled by the sweet thought of revenge. How amazing would it be to take down the gang responsible for so many bad times in her life? And if by some

chance she would get the opportunity to see Victor again
she would not hesitate to end his life. Alicia immediately felt
guilt for her vicious thoughts but rationalized them with the
thought that God wouldn't mind because afterall an eye for an
eye right?

Chapter 12

It only took three days for the Captain and his second in
command to determine that Alicia would be a good fit for the
job. Alicia couldn't be more ecstatic. She drove to the station
as soon as she got the call. These days any excuse to get out
of the house was a good one. The apartment had been tense
ever since Devin had returned from his weekend tryst with his
girlfriend. The siblings had barely spoken to each other. There
were a few words here and there every now and again. "Dinner's ready" or "ill be home late tonight, don't wait up" had
become the norm for verbal exchanges as of late. Devin had
expressed what he really felt about her without the slightest
regard for her feelings, and on top of that he still hadn't even
apologized. Alicia was too grown to play the petty game of
un- forgiveness with her little brother. But though she forgave
him, she had no desire to fraternize with someone who chose
a girl he had only known for 4 months over his own flesh and
blood. In addition to the strained relationship with her brother,
Alicia now found herself feeling weird around Brian. Try as
she might she just wasn't ready to tell him how she felt. She
hoped that this new undercover assignment would take her
mind off Brian long enough to push away her burgeoning feelings. Alicia didn't have time to think about her little brother
or Brian, she had to go to the station and get prepared for her
undercover job.

"Ok so this gang is the real deal, they are very dangerous and ruthless" the captain said. 'Naw you think?' Alicia
thought. "Alicia under no circumstances are you to participate
in crimes with these guys. We simply need you to stay in long
enough to let us know when their next big heroin shipment is
coming in and—"

"Sir if I may," Alicia interrupted, "how do you expect
me to infiltrate these people if I can't engage in any criminal

activity"

"Well I'm glad you asked" he responded snidely. "We will put you undercover as a CPS worker; Bengi Cruz is 4 years old and lives with his grandmother. The grandmother's place also doubles as the head quarters for los víboras. It is an unsafe environment and therefore you as CPS worker Emily Granger, will have to make frequent unscheduled visits"

"Cap am I allowed to do some side work for the gang? I mean these guys are too smart to give in to a woman who won't get her hands dirty. Like you can't believe that they will risk talking about a drop location when I'm around."

"Fine Alicia just don't kill anybody" the captain said shortly.

He was seen as soft by the entire police force. It was only his last name and daddy's political prowess in the city that got him this position. The captain had grown up in the nicest part of Austin in a mansion far away from the ugly side of life. With his mom being a neurologist and his dad being a judge, captain Wells was given everything he asked for as a child, so when out of the blue he asked his dad to make him chief of police that happened too. He had risen through the ranks and just five years after he had completed the police academy he was made captain. Now never having been un-dercover himself, he was heading up the largest heroin bust in Austin's history. But unlike the neophyte captain, Alicia knew the streets. She knew she would have to get creative to get in deep enough so the gang would trust her. She was fueled by a warped sense of justice and revenge. Despite what the captain had authorized she knew she would do whatever she had to do.

In order to get herself into character Alicia wanted a different look. She knew that eventually she would have to talk to her brother so she did it the best way she knew how. She showed up at his girlfriend Rhonda's house and Devin answered the door shirtless.

"What are you doing here Alicia?"

"Well hello to you too brother" Alicia said sarcastically.

"Sorry I just... hi" Devin said attempting to start over. "Let me just put a shirt on, come on in"

'Well I guess that's where his shirt went.' Alicia thought

as a 17 year old Rhonda stumbled out of the bedroom wearing only Devin's baby blue and white checkered button up. "Uh you have to excuse my outfit" Rhonda giggled extending her arm out offering a clumsy handshake. Biting back sarcasm, Alicia shook her hand and properly introduced herself. "Well sorry for popping up on yall un-expectantly I guess you're parents are out of town again? But I actually needed your help. My brother used to talk about you all the time about how you want to be a cosmetologist and how you're really good at doing hair."

"Yeah I do a lil something something… wait did you say he *used* to talk about me" Rhonda said shifting her gaze to Devin.

As much as she wanted to be immature and instigate an argument between the two lustbirds, she came to her little brother's defense. "Well he used to talk about you all the time because *we* used to talk all the time. Ever since the weekend he stayed at your house we've barely said two words to each other"

"I'm so sorry I wasn't trying to come between the two of you" the young girl said innocently staring at the ground. "I mean he still talks about you all the time though, he loves you a lot and misses you, but he's so stubborn ya know?"She said lowering her voice so Devin couldn't hear her.

"Uh well um I need you to perm my hair please… how much do you charge?" Alicia asked changing the subject. Sensing that Alicia and Devin's strained relationship was not up for discussion Rhonda played along and dropped the subject. "Ahh girl you like my sister in law, I got you for free" she said flashing a miniature diamond ring in Alicia's face. Alicia had no words. First Devin had stopped talking to her and now he was marrying this girl and he had just turned sixteen? Alicia chose to keep the conversation on hair.

"O ok thanks, I appreciate that"

"Well I don't want to perm your hair, it's so pretty. You don't wanna mess this up" Rhonda said gazing at Alicia's hair admiringly.

"So how is it going to get straight?"

"Girllll you really are new with hair huh?"Rhonda laughed. "Imma hot comb it and dye it. You would look soooooo hot with blond hair!"

"Haha umm I don't think I'm ready for all that" Alicia said thinking about the need for her to fit into her professional character of a CPS officer. "How bout we dye it light brown instead?"

"Oooh that's hot too! I love it! Devin why you aint never brought your big sis here earlier?" Rhonda gushed. "Look at all this beautiful hair!"

Devin gave a wordless shrug rolling his eyes and changing the channel. By the time Rhonda had finished dying washing, blow drying, and hot combing her hair, Alicia had apologized to Devin. She really didn't know what she was apologizing for but felt that as the older sibling she should go first. Devin followed suit and gave his big sister a hug. "So sis I'll be home a lot more now" Devin smiled. He waited until Rhonda left the room to grab another item for Alicia's hair before continuing. "I mean I love Rhonda and want to be a man but she don't ever have any food over here. She expects me to give her money to buy groceries. Can you believe that?" Devin whispered. Alicia laughed at the irony "Well little brother if you're not ready to make sure she's got everything she needs maybe you're not ready to be the man of the house yet" Alicia said gesturing towards Rhonda's ringed finger. "Aw man she told you?" Devin questioned giving Rhonda the stare down as she re-entered the room carrying a new hair tie. "What' wrong baby did you want me to keep our love secret?" Rhonda asked incredulously. "Of course not baby… come over here and let me give yo fine self some love" Alicia escaped the young couples make out session quietly but with a smile on her face knowing that her and her baby brother's relationship was going to be just fine.

Chapter 13

"Alicia is that you? You look so different"

"Yeah well that was kind of the point" Alicia lightheartedly told Brian. Alicia did look quite different with straight bangs and brown straight hair cascading down to her lower back. She even wore some light lipstick to add a little flair to her beige pantsuit and low black pumps. "Wow well you look amazing as a cps worker… not that you didn't look amazing in your uniform, I mean not that I was checking you out but I—I mean uh…" Brian fumbled with his words. "Well what I'm trying to say is technically we aren't partners right now so maybe we can grab dinner sometime or-"

"Officer Moore can I have a word please" The captain interrupted Brian's clumsy attempt. "Yeah cap ill be in, in a sec. "Alicia responded. "Well Brian we might just have to do that" she said to Brian with a wink. Alicia sashayed to the captains office thinking that maybe her new look was transforming her into a new person- a person that wasn't afraid of falling in love with her hot co-worker.

Alicia drove to the house of Benji with the radio off. Her heart was beating in overdrive and she was afraid if she added the sound of the radio to the pounding sound of her heart beat her ear drums might explode. She felt sorry for little Benji Cruz. This little boy didn't have his mother or father in his life and his young life had already been infiltrated with drugs violence and instability. She made a mental note to have the captain send a real cps officer to aid Benji after the undercover operation was over. For the initial meeting Alicia decided not to wear a wire or a gun. She hoped that the gang would be civil enough for her not to need back up—at least not until she got the necessary information on the heroin drop. Just as Alicia pulled up to the house she suddenly got a sinking feeling in her gut. The same feeling she had gotten when Marcus pulled up to the curb of his house bleeding so many years ago. She knew he was going to die in that moment. She shook her head hoping that this déjà vu was not a foreshadowing of more bad events to come.

"A yo Victor! Some black chick out here on the porch bro!" Alicia heard a young man yell through the screen door. 'Victor… Victor Cruz as in Binji Cruz's father??? How could I have been so stupid what was I thinking?' Alicia thought as she tried to calm her breathing down as panic crept up her spine. The screen door screeched open noisily. "What you want lady?" The rude bald headed tattooed man asked at the door. "Chico, Chico, Chico that is no way you talk to a lady papi" Victor said with his trademark smooth talking. He still had those gorgeous eyes, those eyes that could seduce you

and lie to you at the same time. Pull it together pull it together Alicia thought. "Hello sir, my name is Emily Granger and I am here to speak with the guardian of Benji Cruz... A Mrs. Rosalie
Perez, I believe" Alicia said putting on her glasses and referring to her notes for affect. "Well I'm his father what's this about?" Victor asked.

"Well sir I am with child protective services and we have reason to believe that this boy is not being properly cared for"

"Well I can assure you he is"

"Sir I need to speak to Mrs. Perez"

"She took Benji to the park. The only reason I didn't have my son was because I was in prison but that's why im down here getting myself together so me and my son can move back up north."

Alicia wondered if "getting himself together" consisted of helping out in the gangs largest drug shipment in Austin's history.

"Ok sir I understand that, but I do have to speak with the legal guardian. If she is not here I can come back in a couple of days. If I can't catch up with her soon I will be forced to take the child."

With that statement Alicia exited the house.For a moment she considered backing out of the undercover operation altogether. She didn't know if she trusted herself with a gun in Victor Cruz's presence. Some part of her wanted to take that chance. If she finished the operation, great, if Victor Cruz accidently got shot with a bullet from her pistol, no big deal. She felt guilty about the weird pot of thoughts of justice and revenge that was swirling around in her head, but decided to see how things played out. "Vengeance is Mine..." kept flashing past her mind's eye on the long drive back to the police station. Though she couldn't quite remember where she had heard that quote suddenly she was calm.

Chapter 14

Alicia was back on the job a couple days later and back to the Cruz home just a she had promised. She had decided to visit early in the day in hopes that Victor would still be sleeping off a hangover. But she had guessed wrong. "Hola chica bonita" a shirtless and pantless Victor said opening the door. His old boxer shorts did nothing to hide his apparent excitement about her arrival. No matter though, she had dressed extra nice today, curled her long light brown hair and she even made sure a little cleavage was showing atop of her royal purple blouse. She was still prepared to throw Victor off as much as possible. "Mr. Cruz can I come in and see Benji please?" Alicia asked sternly but with a touch of sweetness. Victor was more than happy to oblige her. Stepping in the house she chose to ignore the faint smell of weed emanating from a closed bedroom door at the far end of the narrow hallway in the three bedroom house. The smell meant that Victor's companions might be in the room talking about the big shipment and she would be one step closer to getting that big drug bust she was really here for. "So Benji sleeps in here with me" Victor said as he showed her the master bedroom of the house. "Are you sure you're not just trying to get me alone in your room" Alicia giggled. She felt him staring at her round backside as she entered the small space.

The cutest little boy she'd ever seen emerged from under the covers as he heard them enter the room. "Hi Benji I'm your case worker Emily, you're not in any trouble I just want you to show me around the place a little bit" Alicia said squatting down so that she could be eye level with the little boy. Victor nodded his approval and Benji took Alicia by the hand and began to lead her around. "Well this is me and my daddy's room and then out here is where my daddy's friends play cards, then over here is where my grandma cooks and this room is where she sleeps and this room is...." Benji stopped short. Alicia ignored the look of murder on Victor's face and asked Benji about the room he previously neglected to introduce her to. Only in the innocent way of a child Benji expressed that it was "daddy's special room" and that he was forbidden to go in there. Alicia had found her way in. After sending Benji back to his room, she sat on the couch and filled out some nonsensical paper work. When she felt that the moment was right, she got up and eased close to Victor. "So Mr. Cruz what goes on in your 'special room'?" she asked as innocently as she could muster. "Look mami I can't have you taking my son from me, he's all I got." "Well then let's talk about what you and I can do for each other" she responded.

After much more forced flirting and about 30 minutes of extra conversation, Alicia was happy with the deal she had made with Victor. She would over look the drugs in the house and let Victor keep Benji if he cut her in on a small piece of the operation. Victor agreed to give her some additional cash every now and then if she agreed to go on a few dates with him. Alicia was doing pretty well staying in character but she almost lost it when the term "dates" was used. "Dates" were what her mom used to call them. She shuddered at the thought of it but consoled herself by knowing that if Victor tried anything, this time she would have a gun to protect herself that she was more than happy to use.

She ran into trouble on her third visit. It seemed like the gang was out in full force. It was the mean man from before, Chico who answered the door to her. After staring her down evilly before letting her in, he voiced his concern to the room. "Yo Victor I don't trust this chick. My sister practically lives at that cps office and I always take her down there. How come I've never seen you in that office Emily?" He directed his question toward Alicia. "Sir with all do respect, please allow me to do this visit properly. I'm trying to make sure that Benji is well taken care of. All I am trying to do is my job. "And lady with all do respect you aint answer my question?" Chico said and all ears in the room perked up. "Ok fine" She said keeping her composure. "Do you want to see my case load?" She asked pulling out a bulky manila folder from her leather bound briefcase. I'm fresh out of college, and I'm new to the company so they overloaded me with a bunch of cases, so I'm never in the office."

"Ok Chico she gave you an answer now let this pretty lady check on Benji like she's supposed to, Benji come out here " he yelled.

"Naw I still don't trust her but how about this. How bout you do something for me?" Chico said to her.

"I'm not doing anything illegal"

"You're already doing something illegal I know you have been getting some of our money" Chico retorted. "Here's what I need for you to do. I need you to get my sister's kids returned to her. She has my two little nieces, they're twins and they keep trying to take them away"

"Well I'll have to look into it, but I may not be able to help you with that."

"Well then I'll have to call your boss and get you fired then won't I."

"I'll see what I can do."

She called the CPS agency early the next morning from the police station. "Officer Moore I can't just send two kids back to these conditions" The frustrated lady on the phone told her.

"Yes ma'am I know it's a lot of red tape but-"

"It's not about the red tape" the woman said, cutting Alicia off. "This mother is a heroin addict. We were called in after a neighbor called the cops because they were left alone all night. The babies are only 17 months. When we got there they were both hungry and very smelly if you know what I mean."

Alicia's stomach dropped. "Well ma'am I promise it will only be temporary" Alicia assured her.

"Officer, let me ask you something. Would you leave your children in the care of a heroin addict for even 5 minutes? Temporary is too long for these children. They may not be from a wealthy family but we care for all of them just the same." And with that the woman hung up. Alicia only had one card left to play. She had to go to Captain Wells and ask him to override the concerned cps agent and have the children returned to Monica. It was one of the hardest things she ever had to do but she knew she would make it right, but in the meantime she prayed that God would keep them safe.

Chapter 15

For the first couple visits to the Cruz residence Alicia had been driving her own car, a 2007 vanilla colored Buick. But after her test of loyalty she didn't want to take the chance of anyone involved with los víboras spotting her car around town so she started taking the bus instead to do her weekly visits. One day after a visit the bus she usually took to return home was 45 minutes late and the street lights were beginning to flicker on. She didn't want to be around a whole lot of víboras when it got completely dark so she decided to start walking. Alicia forgot how much she loved walking. Long walks in the cool breeze always helped calm her down no matter how stressful the day. She only planned to walk to the next bus stop but soon she found that in her enjoyment she walked further than she had intended to and it was getting dark fast. She hadn't brought her gun with her, but she did have mace in her purse and a sheathed straight razer tucked securely between her ample breasts.

Oh great, she thought as she looked up the street and saw an unkempt bunch of three guys smoking by the rail-road tracks. *Just put your head down and keep walking* Alicia thought as she hurriedly buttoned the top button of her crimson blouse. "Hey girl whatchu doin out here alone?" One of the men slurred as she neared them. Another offered her a drink from his brown bagged beverage. They made their way over to the side of the street she was walking on. "Hey don't you hear us talking to u trick?!" yelled the third one as he lunged for her arm. The man was not prepared for her quick reflexes. In a 10 second span of time she kicked him, punched him, and maced him in the face. The men attacked her simultaneously. Again she remembered the training she had received from the police academy and coupled it with the tremendous amount of experience she gathered in the school of hard knocks. She fought defensively like Floyd Mayweather, always avoiding a hit to the face. Just as she had dodged a punch and turned to dash away she heard the sound of a gun cocking. "You move and I'll blow your head off" said the guy she first maced, now walking with new confidence with the small cheap gun in his hand. "Put your hands up" he screamed menacingly. When she did the two other guys took their opportunity to get a few punches in that caused Alicia to cry out and fall to her knees in pain. The man with the gun slowly approached her. Before he could do anything blinding high beams from a big black truck came from the right side of the tracks. Brian hopped out of the car before anyone's eyes could adjust to what was happening. In a few quick moves Brian had leveled all three men and removed the bullets from the gun. "Come on Alicia lets go" Brian said scooping her up gently and tenderly placing her in the passenger seat. He sped into the night leaving the three dizzy wana be thugs behind. Unknown to Brian and Alicia though, the whole scene was being watched by suspecting eyes. Chico followed Alicia on her walk. He was careful to keep a good distance and in his opinion it seemed that the woman was oblivious to the rough neighborhoods she so carelessly walked though. Nothing interesting happened for about two miles so Chico was about to turn back until he saw Alicia get into the altercation with the three men. The speed and ferocity of her kicks and punches astonished him. There was no way this little woman worked for child protective services. Chico witnessed the man who saved her. He didn't get a good look at his face but Chico was able to get a picture of half of his license plate number as the truck speed off in the distance. He pocketed his phone and turned back towards the Cruz house.

"Hey, thanks for helping me out, but you know I had it under control, Brian" Alicia said between labored breaths in the speeding truck. "Yeah I'm sure you did have it under control" Brian spat finding himself growing angry. "You know what Alicia? I'll drop you off at your apartment and then you won't have to worry about me anymore. When we see each other at work it'll be strictly professional. "Wait…" Alicia interjected, "no you wait Alicia! All I do is try to help you; can't you see that I love you?" Brian asked his eyes pleading that she'd reciprocate his feelings as they pulled up to her apartment building. Alicia said nothing as she slowly stepped down out of the big truck. She had a feeling that Brian thought of her as more than a friend and she suspected that she thought of him as more than a friend too. That is why ever since she told him her story in the apartment a while ago, she spent her time consumed with this undercover mission. She hadn't even seen her little brother in a few weeks. It was apparent that he wanted to live with Rhonda and it was just easier to not get a fight started between them. Alicia was usually never the one to back down from a fight but the insatiable desire for revenge on Victor Cruz had been clouding her judgment lately. Because of the awkward silence after Brian professed his love, he decided to bow out gracefully and leave, but the defeat was only momentary because Alicia came to her senses before he turned the vehicle out of her complex. "Brian!"

Alicia screamed. "I'm so sorry. I just….. I've been dealing with a lot lately" she began fumbling with her words as Brian rolled his window down and slowed to a stop. "Well Brian what I'm trying to say is, do you wanna come up?"

Upon entering the threshold of the apartment Alicia aggressively began kissing his lips and unbuttoning his shirt. "Whoa whoa whoa!" Brian exclaimed. "I'm not here for that Alicia!" "What?" Alicia asked confused. "But you said that you loved me… this is the second time you've turned me down, now I'm really beginning to think that you really are gay!" Alicia spat at him shaking her head in disgust. "Look Alicia I don't appreciate all the name calling because I won't have sex with you, but I understand because I get that a lot. But what you need to understand is that sex and love are not equals. Sex does not mean that you love someone and love does not mean you have sex with someone." "What the world are you talking about Brian?" Asked a very vexed Alicia with hands on her hips. "Ok so it goes like this" Brian said taking a seat on the sofa. "So you ever heard of John 3:16" he asked Alicia. She shook her head no. "Well it says 'For God so loved the world that He gave His only begotten Son, that whosover believeth in Him shall not perish but have everlasting life.' That is real love, do you know what I'm saying Alicia?" "Well what I get is that you want me to believe in someone that has allowed me to go through so much pain and suffering in my life. Do you know what I've been through Brian! How would this great big loving God of yours allow those things to happen to me?" She screamed at him.

"Look Alicia there is nothing bad in God. Do you think that there are evil forces at work?"

"What like the devil? Demons versus angels and stuff like that?"

"Yeah like that."

"Yeah I do think there is a Heaven and Hell if that's what you're asking."

"Well the devil has made it his job to try to destroy people and totally ruin good situations. On the other hand God sent His son Jesus Christ to this earth in the form of a baby to grow up and eventually die for the people of this earth in order that we could have life and a great life at that. God never did all of those horrible things to you. He's the One trying to heal the pain in you that was caused by what happened."

"How do I know that you're not lying to me?"

"It's your decision. But if you decide to follow the teachings and guidance of Jesus Christ, you've got to have faith."

Something unexplainable gripped Alicia at that moment, and she ran outside the door to get some fresh air. She felt dizzy and rigid at the same time. She was filled with uncertainty yet had the feeling that she had been waiting for this moment her whole life. She caught her breath, and then went back inside.

"Brian I wanna do it right now" she said. "Alicia come on I thought we already discussed sex…"

"Not that, please don't flatter yourself, I want to give my life to Christ, how do I do it?" she asked.

"Well Romans 10:9-10, in the Bible tells us 'that if you confess with your mouth that Jesus is Lord and believe in your heart that God raised Him from the dead, you will be saved. For with the heart one believes and is justified, and with the mouth one confesses and is saved.'

"Ok so is there some sort of magical feeling and special words you want me to repeat"

"No magic, just faith… I'll give you and God some alone time." Brian softly stated before quietly exiting the apartment. After a moment Alicia began to speak.

"Ok so God I'm not good at this but since you are almighty I'm pretty sure You'll know what I'm trying to say. Well um what I mean is I'm sorry and I don't want to be hurt and angry all the time anymore. I want to live right. I don't want to live the way I used to. I see a difference in Brian and I want to be able to see that difference in my life. Uh basically I want You… I need You I know that Jesus Christ is Lord and that God You raised Him from the dead… just help me to live for You from now on… lead the way and help me to follow You Lord. In the name of Jesus I ask this….. Uh Amen and thanks"

Chapter 16

Things were going great for Alicia, she was a new Christian, she could admit that she was falling for a man, and she had Victor and his gang right where she wanted them. Alicia expertly took advantage of Victor's lust for flesh, she flirted with him every time she paid a visit to little Benji. Soon they began going on dates regularly. She happily continued to accept his invitations because of the fact that he gave her a little money from his drug business. She did this because even if the drug bust didn't come to fruition, a jury would be able to nail him on giving money to an undercover officer. But she desperately needed the drug bust to happen because she wanted Victor to spend the rest of his life rotting in a small prison cell. She had to admit that she kind of felt bad for Benji though. If Victor was thrown in prison then Benji would have to be cared for by his grandmother, but the woman looked about 70. Victor's mom had him late in life. It would be a shame for Benji to be thrust into the foster system. The presence of Victor still made her skin crawl but she had become an excellent actress, especially when, two nights ago Victor had kissed her on the lips. When she got home she threw up three different times. How could she forgive the man who raped her and the man who had killed her best friend- her first love, Marcus so long ago? But today she wanted to call Brian; she had been so busy with the case that they didn't have much time to spend together lately.

"Hello," his silky smooth voice answered

"Hey Brian" Alicia answered shyly

"So how's it going with you little lady?"

"Well, it could be better but it could also be worse ya know what I mean?"

"I do, I know exactly what you mean."

"So Brian I'd like to see you tonight at my apartment if you're not busy."

"Yeah well I don't think that such a good idea, ya know seeing as how you can't keep your hands off of me when I'm in your apartment" Brian joked.

"On scouts honor I just want to invite you over to play scrabble."

"O is that what that call it nowadays?" he asked playfully "I'll see you at 7."

Brian arrived at 6:45 on the dot. Alicia opened the door to a freshly cleaned apartment that emanated the bright sounds of Elle Varner's song 'Refill' and the fresh smells of catfish, broccoli and wild rice. On the table was an open game of scrabble. "Oh so you really weren't kidding" Brian said as he entered the apartment with a big smile on his face. "Did I ever tell you that you have a beautiful smile" Alicia complimented him. That only made him cheese even harder. "Did I ever tell you that I would love to kiss you" Brian asked. Alicia laughed him off. It was a little too soon to start kissing another man seeing as how her last kiss from a man caused her to throw up repeatedly. As usual, once the pair got settled in conversation flowed easily between them. Brian complimented her cooking several times. "Ok so I think it's time for scrabble" Alicia declared as she cleared the empty plates from the table. Brian reached into the bag of letters and pulled the letter A, which signified that he would go first. He got a great selection of letters and was able to put the word 'chime' on the board to start them off. "Great!" Alicia said," I have the perfect words for this." "Hey now, you can only put down one word at a time, rookie," Brian objected. "Just trust me," Alicia responded. She began digging for more and more letters out of the bag. She began spelling a word underneath the letter I. She placed down L-O-V-E-U-T-O-O. "Triple word score!" she said excitedly, "that gives me 24 points and the lead." "No" Brian said staring deeply in her eyes, "That gives you a lifetime." He leaned in to kiss her but they were interrupted by an angry knock at the door. "Detective Moore it's officer Suarez! Could you come to the door please" A raspy female voice yelled through the door. Alicia hurried over, disappointed that the moment was ruined. She opened the door to a stern looking member of her unit and her deshelved looking little brother. "What'd he do Tammy?" Alicia asked with concern "I caught him eyeing the Sears outside of the mall pretty hard. He had tools in his hand. I thought since I know you I'd just bring him here and save you the embarrassment and me the paperwork"

"Thanks officer Suarez." Alicia said after a few moments through clenched jaws. "I'll take it from here." Officer Suarez wasn't very far down the steps before she could hear the yells of Alicia's strong disapproval toward Devin. "Devin what were you thinking? How could you do this?!"

"Look you were the one who kicked me out of the house Alicia; I was just going to get Rhonda a present."

"Devin you were going to break into Sears and risk your record and your freedom just to get your little girlfriend a present" Alicia was dumfounded.

"Hey Rhonda is not just my little girlfriend we love each other and you need to respect that… and who is this?" Devin asked pointing towards Brian.

"We're not talking about me" Alicia said sternly. "We are talking about you. You're a child Devin, you need to come back home."

"That's exactly it Alicia! I'm not a little baby anymore, I'm growing up, I'm in love, I have a family now and…"

"Ok I'll start treating you more like a man now since you're growing up and….. Wait why did you say that you have a family now?" Alicia asked incredulously.

"Well sis, I… I'm going to be a dad"

Chapter 17

The captain had been droning on and on for what seemed like hours in the station about the next step in the drug sting. "Alicia have you gotten any information about when this drop is going to take place. It seems to me you and Victor have gotten pretty close."

"Sir respectfully, what is that supposed to mean? I'm trying my best to get the information, it may take time though."

"How much more time do you think you need it's been over 6 months?"

"Sir if I could just get a little more time to—"

"No Alicia, excuse me, I mean *Emily* do what you need to do, get into character and drive this home for us! This is taking way too much time don't make me regret putting you on this assignment."

You mean don't make me look bad Alicia thought, but instead of speaking her mind she simply responded with a "yes sir."

"So I need the drop location in three days time Alicia. We have expended enough resources on this and the mayor is burning my britches about the drug issue. You need to make an unscheduled visit tonight."

Alicia didn't want to visit Victor tonight, she and Brian had started dating exclusively for the last couple months and she'd much rather be snuggled up on his couch watching a new action flick. But, nonetheless she texted Brian to let him know she would be unavailable to come over since she had to get the location. Brian asked her to send the address of where she would be because he was a little nervous about where the night might lead.

"Daddy, daddy, Emily's here" little Benji yelled out gleefully. Over the past 6 months he had really taken a liking to her and would always give her a big hug when she came to make visits. "A what's up mami?" asked a shirtless Victor as he approached the door. Alicia cringed as she looked at all of his gang tattoos. She couldn't help but wonder if one of those teardrops under his eye was meant to signify his murder of Marcus so long ago. She quickly shook the thought away. "Hello little man, and how are you Victor?" Alicia asked cordially as she entered the house. After the quick visit with Benji was over Victor suggested that his mother take Benji out to the park to play. His mother agreed, leaving Alicia and Victor all alone. Alicia didn't have much time to waste since the whole unit was depending on her so she had to act fast before Victor's mother and son returned. "So Victor I've really been enjoying the money you have giving me, thank you" she said lightly touching his chest. "Well there's more where that came from mami" he responded. "How can I ever get some of that?" she asked seductively. "There's a couple ways I can think of, step one is you taking your clothes off." He said. "Whoa Victor I'm not that easy" she laughed pushing his hand away "but when do you think I'll have this money."

"Well I can give you a couple thousand right now" he responded.

"Victor I'm not a prostitute" Alicia said pretending to be offended. I thought we were partners. My office really wants to take Benji away from you but I haven't let them. And for that I wanna be cut in" she affirmed.

"Cut in to what?"

"Cut in to the big payout, don't think I have'nt noticed you and your boys scrambling around a lot more lately. Something big is going down and I want in."

"Do you see Chico and the guys I hang with? They'll never agree to you getting a cut without doing anything."

"Well let me be a lookout or something... I promise I'll earn my keep" Alicia said running her hands down his chiseled abs until she let them linger expectantly down near his crotch. Now she had gotten his attention. She felt his member rising instinctively through his pants. She wanted him to think with the little brain instead of the big one in his head. "Look just tell me where to meet you baby and then you won't even have to pick me up" she said in between soft neck kisses. It didn't take much persuasion for Victor to provide the main details of the drop to Alicia. Now that she had gotten her information she removed her hand from his crotch and continued kissing him. "A yo mami why'd you stop that's was feeling good, but I want something else now. You thought that information I just gave you was for free?" He asked with a look of fire in his eyes. He had the same look in his eyes when he had cornered her in the restroom outside of the prom all those years ago. "Wait a minute Victor, do you know how much trouble I'll get in if my boss finds out we slept together?" Alicia asked trying to stall.

"Yeah probably about the same amount of trouble you'll get in for taking my money" Victor said smiling as he began to unbuckle his khaki pants. Seeing what was happening Alicia's heart rate sped up. She couldn't go through this again there was no way she would let it happen this time. She still had the small knife tucked away discretely in her bra. If he made it that far he would be in for a painful surprise. "Ok just wait a minute..." Alicia said quickly getting up from the couch. "Wait for what?" Victor asked licking his lips. "Well we don't... we don't have a condom or anything Victor"

"So" he responded firmly pushing her back down on the worn out couch. Alicia quickly reached her hand down her shirt to grab the knife but before she could grab it they were interrupted by a frantic knocking on the door.

"Ms. Granger, are you in there?!" A man's voice yelled outside the door. Irritated, Victor got off of her slowly and looked out the window to see who was out there. "Yo you know a tall black dude... I know you aint dealing with no other guy" Victor spat at Alicia. Alicia didn't know who was outside the door but she hoped it was a fellow officer that she knew or better yet, Brian. "It's probably my boss checking up on me" she answered. "Please put your shirt on before you open the door so I don't get fired" she continued. Victor walked to the door shirtless but changed his mind at the last minute and put back on his shirt and buckled his pants all the way up. "Emily what's your boss's name?" Victor asked with a sly look on his face. Knowing that this was a test, Alicia answered without hesitation. "His name is James Williams and he's gonna be pissed at me, I was supposed to have my weekly reports on his desk before 5! I've gotta go, Victor" Alicia said. She hoped that she guessed the correct cover name. She remembered that Brian talked about enjoying the James Bond movies. But if it wasn't Brian outside than her cover was blown already. It seemed like ages before Victor opened the door.

"Hello sir my name is James I'm looking for one of my cps workers, Ms. Emily Granger, she was supposed to do a quick visit here than report back before the close of the business day, you know gotta get this information out to the state" Brian chuckled lightly. Alicia was relieved that it was him and even more pleased that they were apparently on the same wavelength. "Is that so?" Victor asked still slightly skeptical. "Ah sir I'm so sorry, I totally forgot to get those reports over to you in time, the visit took a little longer than I intended." Alicia said as she came to the door with several papers sloppily gathered in her hands. "Thank you Mr. Cruz and I should be back in about a month to visit Benji" Alicia said shaking Victor's hand before quickly rushing out the door. Brian turned to walk to his car but paused to think about what a real boss would do. "Oh sir I'm so sorry about Emily, we pride ourselves on being professional and I assure you that she will be written up for her choice of outfit today. I'd be more than happy to change case workers for you Mr. Cruz" Brian added for effect. The pair left quickly in separate cars before Victor could ask too many more questions.

"Hey Cap I got the drop location and its going down soon" Alicia said over the phone to the captain as soon as she was far enough away from the Cruz house for Victor to see her.

"We've got a problem" the captain responded "we just arrested Victor's second in command."

"Chico?" Alicia asked. She already knew that the captain was undeserving of his position, but she didn't think that he was inept enough to arrest an integral part of the drug shipment days before the bust was supposed to go down. "How could you do this to me, you know what I've had to go through for this to happen perfectly!" Alicia screamed at him and ended the call still shaking from her close encounter with Victor. What scared her wasn't the attempted rape instead she was terrified at what she was about to do. She had the strong feeling that if Brian hadn't of knocked on the door when he did she would of pulled out her knife and blacked out. She said a silent prayer of thanks to God for preventing that from happening. Alicia was fully aware about what the Bible says about murderers and those who don't forgive others. She didn't want to be either of those types of people but she couldn't help but get a fire in her gut when she was around Victor. She felt like a snake waiting quietly in the grass until it was time for her to strike and exact her revenge. She had shared how she felt about Victor to Brian many months ago. He sympathized with her pain but he urged her to forgive him and try to want the best for him. Alicia remembered freaking out on Brian and asking him why he was siding with Victor. She always remembered the calm assured response that Brian gave her "Jesus gave up everything for you and you didn't deserve it. You need to forgive this man so that you can move on." Alicia hadn't understood what he meant by those words and she feared that she wouldn't be able to control herself if she was alone with Victor… and a gun.

Alicia quieted her inner thoughts as she came upon the police station. She saw Brian's black truck already parked in the front. As she slowed down to execute the left turn into the lot she froze as she noticed a familiar man making his way out of the building with a flurry of curse words flying out of his mouth. *Why are they letting Chico go now?* she thought. This was the second time in a span of fifteen minutes that Captain Wells had almost blown her cover. She hoped that Chico didn't see her pull up to the station but when the cursing stopped abruptly, Alicia feared that he had. She parked and

opened the car door to tell her fellow officers to keep Chico
locked up so that he wouldn't be able to tell Victor. But, she
was interrupted.

"Hey take him in back in here we've still got some
questions to ask him" Captain Wells said as he rushed out of
the stations glass door and hurried down the steps. "I need my
phone call Chico yelled back I aint answering any questions
until I get my phone call"

Alicia knew that they wouldn't be able to hold Chico too
much longer without giving him his phone call. One phone
call to Victor meant that the past 6 months and the strained
relationship with her brother would all be in vain. Alicia sped
back out of the parking lot, tires screeching along the way.

"Brian" Alicia said after he answered on the first ring.
"We need to set this meeting up tonight and I need your help."

Chapter 18

As much as Brian hated to agree to it, their only play was
to send Alicia back in, in hopes that she could convince Victor
to move the time of the drop up; And if she could keep him
away from his phone. She did 90 on the highway all the way
to Victor's house. Despite the speeding, Alicia was unable to
arrive before the dreaded phone call was made.

"You have a call from Austin prison do you accept the
charges?" an automated voice echoed through the phone. "Yes
I accept the charges" Victor responded.

"A Victor I told you she was a cop man!"

"Who Emily?"

"Yeah man! I followed her one night she was walking
home. Some guy picked her up about a mile away from your
crib and I seen that same truck, same license plate in the parking lot at the police station man."

Victor said nothing for a moment. "Thanks bro I'll take
care of it" and he quickly hung up the phone as he heard
someone running up to his door.

"Victor!" Alicia yelled through the screen door. "Victor
hurry I've got some bad news." He came to the door. "What's
up mami? You come back for more" he said reaching for her
arm.

"Victor, Chico just got arrested."

"How do you know?" He asked.

"You and Benji are not my only case" she informed him. "One of the mothers of the other child I visit was just booked on suspicion of DUI and I wanted to check on her…anyway that's not the point." She continued. "The point is I saw them bringing Chico in."

"Do you know what they busted him for?" Victor asked.

"No I didn't wait around to see. I came straight here, but all I know is if he talks you can say goodbye to all the money we were going to be making on this deal!"

"We?" Victor asked.

"Yes we" Alicia confirmed "I can give you up at anytime"

"Is that so?" Victor said with ferocity as he got over to her and grabbed her roughly by the neck. "Are you threatening me?"

"Get your hands off of me" She said back with equal ferocity.

"Ooh I like that you aint even scared mami" he said before he released his hold on her neck.

"I'm trying to make sure all of wind up ok. All you have to do is call up your connect and tell them to meet us at the spot in 30 minutes. Afterward we can come back here and scoop up Benji then head out of town for a couple of days until it cools off."

"I don't think Chico is going to talk"

"Ok, but if he does talk, we all lose out on a lot of money and we both go to prison. Please make the call." She pleaded.

Alicia didn't know what he had told his contacts but Victor was able to move the time up relatively easily and within five minutes he and Alicia had loaded the money in the trunks of their two cars and left to get to the location. They arrived on the corner of 52nd and Burdine just as it started to sprinkle. Alicia got out of her car but this time with her gun placed in the small of her back. One by one 4 other cars arrived, and several nefarious looking characters stepped out of the vehicles. Alicia and Victor got out of the car to meet them.

"Is this her?" The biggest man asked Victor

"Yeah this is the cop" he responded. "You got my

product?"

"Sure do. You got my money?" the large man covered in tattoos confirmed as he moved toward Alicia gun drawn. Alicia looked at Victor in disbelief, but was unable to say anything before the big man grabbed her roughly by the hair. The fierce yank on her hair bun sent all of her hair spilling out of its band. "You know what I'm gonna do for you cop?" The man asked rhetorically, "I'm not gonna kill you. I'm gonna have you work for me." He said running his dirty hand down the flawless mocha skin of her face and neck.

"Hey T I don't like the feeling of this" One of the other men interuppted. "Where's Chico, I thought he was supposed to be here. "Yo are you setting me up! Are you working with her?!" T yelled as he turned his pistol on Victor.

Before Victor could answer the group turned as 5 police cars came careening towards them. T and his boys were able to squeeze off a couple of rounds before hopping back into their cars but Alicia and Victor ran to retreat in the abandoned flea market around the corner.

"Yo mami get down!" Victor screamed but instead of finding a demure female diving for cover, he looked up to find Alicia pointing a gun at him. "Yo Emily what are you doing?" he asked clearly surprised. "I really wasn't gonna sell you to that dude" he lied. "I was just buying us some time." Alicia shook her head at Victor surprised that he was still trying to use charm to get out of a situation. As the rain poured harder and harder Alicia's hair appeared darker and the trademark curls of her youth sprang forth. Suddenly Victor's face grew pale. "Alicia" he said. There was no need to ask her, he remembered. Alicia cocked the gun. "Mami we was young. You know all that stuff we did didn't mean nothin."

"Shut up!" Alicia screamed at him. "We didn't do anything! You raped me and you killed Marcus!"

"Hey that only happened cuz-"Victor started.

"Shut up I said! If only you knew how you ruined my life!" She raised the gun from his chest to his head. "Get in here" she said gesturing toward the open door behind them "Get on your knees" Alicia told him as she wiped the angry tears streaming down her face. "You... you made me a murderer!"

"Yo I aint make you kill nobody! And you don't have to kill me now" Victor said.

"But you're right I'll take responsibility for the life I took. But I…. I just didn't want your baby growing inside of me!" Alicia screamed bitterly with spittle spewing from her mouth.

"So what you killed my kid?" Victor asked now becoming angry.

"Yes I had an abortion. I'm not proud of it. Hey!" Alicia yelled as Victor tried to leave his knees. "Keep your hands in front of me" she demanded. Victor grew more bold and instead of begging for his life he began sneering at her and hurling Spanish curses at her a mile a minute. For some reason that reminded her of the last Bible study Brian had with her. They had studied a passage in Matthew 18 where Jesus was telling one of His disciples that He should forgive someone 70 time 7 times.

Time seemed to stand still as Alicia reached in her pocket and dialed her captain. I've got Victor Cruz in my custody. We are on the bottom floor of the market across from your location" Alicia said hanging up the phone. "I forgive you" Alicia said quietly. "What?" Victor asked. "I said I forgive you" she said speaking louder.

She managed to not shoot Victor. When the Captain came to arrest him she just stared blankly at him as he was led away, all the while threatening to kill her or ruin her life. Even with him hurling homicidal threats her way she was able to smile, because she knew she was different now. Jesus Christ had changed her. 10 years ago, and even 6 months ago she would have killed him while she had the chance. She smiled because she realized bitterness no longer had control of her life anymore.

Chapter 19

Alicia was suspended without pay for a week following the big drug bust. She thought that was fair, considering she put a lot of lives at risk because she did not inform the captain about her previous gang ties. Captain Wells would never fire her though because, thanks to her he was able to receive the glory for making the biggest heroin bust the city had seen in over 20 years. They were able to seize over 15 kilos and make

4 arrests, and only one perp was killed. It was a man by the name of Terrell Waters, but he was known in the drug world as simply 'T'. As soon as the operation was over Alicia stood true to her promise and within the week Benji Cruz had a real CPS agent assigned to him, and the twins girls were once again taken away from Monica. Alicia said a silent prayer of thanks for His protection over all of the little children, and for His amazing protection of her.

Chapter 20

"So…" was all Brian said when he entered her apartment a month after the incident with Victor. "Yes my love" she responded smiling. As soon as he turned away from her words, immediately Alicia knew something had changed for them.

"Go ahead. I knew this was too good to be true. Just get it over with and breakup with me already" Alicia said with an even tone.

"Look it's not that simple, I mean… I don't really know how to explain it-"

"Sure, I do… Let me guess you found somebody else. If we are meant to be it'll come back around, it's not you it's me? Choose a cliché Brian!" Alicia demanded, her anger growing.

"No it's none of those" Brian promised reaching for her hand. "God told me that our relationship is on hold for now. When He tells me the time is right I will ask you to be my wife. Maybe God knows if we stay together now we'll mess up and have sex, or maybe God is protecting us from some-thing else down the road. But Alicia Renee Moore you will be my wife one day. He just hasn't told me when."

"Hold up 1 second. So you're saying God told you all of this? Did He also tell you the people we are supposed to date in between before our hearts meet once again to be joined in Holy matrimony?" Alicia asked sarcastically as she forcefully removed his hand from hers. "You should just go" she added as she moved to the doorway to lead him out.

"Wait" Brian said "we are not supposed to date any-one else in between Alicia. We have been promised to each other."

Alicia's head was spinning and she was more than happy to kick Brian out of her house. *How can a loving God bring someone that amazing into my life just to take him away again she thought.* She tried to search her brain to figure out why that was and in the recesses of her mind she stumbled across a memory. A hidden jewel that the pastor of the new church she started attending told the congregation once. He said God gives and God takes away. Maybe this is what her pastor meant. Maybe God gives us things only for a period of time and especially exactly when we need them. She realized she would just have to be content until God told Brian it was the right time for her to be his wife. This of course was tough for her because she had always been independent. After her dad left and her mom was murdered it was her calling the shots. She was always the boss. Now was the perfect practice on how to be submissive to her husband if and when that day came. *But thank You Jesus that I don't have a husband to submit to now because I am not ready for that.* She prayed with a smile.

Chapter 21

It had been 2 months since Brian had broken up with her and now Devin called to tell her he was coming by the apartment to talk to her. "I know we haven't really got to talk lately but Rhonda is 7 months pregnant now."

Alicia remained silent. "You're not going to yell at me or anything?" Devin asked incredulously. Alicia was too weary to argue with Devin. "Congratulations little brother," she said weakly. "I know you'll be a good daddy." With all the stress that came with the undercover operation, Alicia never got the chance to discuss the bomb Devin dropped on her that he and Rhonda were expecting. In fact she avoided it.

"Listen a baby's a blessing. Of course I wanted you to wait but now there is no taking this back. Your little gift from God is on his way. And that means a lot of respon-sibility-"

"I know sis I've got already got a job lined up for after schools and weekends and Rhonda's parents said they'd-"

"No that's not what I meant Dev" Alicia interrupted gently. "I mean that raising your little man is a special responsibility. You are charged with making him a man. Just promise me one thing Dev" she continued.

"What's that sis?"

"Promise me that you'll teach him the value of a woman. Make sure he knows that a woman is a person too, and not just some object for him to use. Make sure he knows that a woman should be respected even during the times she doesn't respect herself." With that Alcia got up and went into her bedroom and shut the door softly. A few seconds later she heard a soft rap on the door.

"You can come in Devin" she said just after she brushed away the few tears that had fallen on her face. "Alicia I never told you I was having a boy. How did you know?"

"I've been texting Rhonda for a few months now" Alicia admitted. "I don't care how often we disagree, I'll always love you and i'll always be your big sister." The loving smile he gave her before he walked out of the room and closed the door behind him meant more than his words ever could. Alicia knew they were good now.

She had been praying for her brother every day straight for six weeks now and she had faith that it was only a matter of time before he too decided to get saved. Until then she was looking forward to picking him and Rhonda up next Sunday to go to the 12 noon church service they finally agreed to attend. She walked over to the cute kitten's calendar hanging on her closet door to write a reminder to pick them up at 11am. She smiled as she looked at the message for the reminder for next Saturday: "Meet Brian at First Christian church for pre-engagement counseling."

www.ingramcontent.com/pod-product-compliance
Lightning Source LLC
Chambersburg PA
CBHW070400120726
47909CB00008B/2934